Once Upon a Tide

Tony Mitton

⭐

Illustrated by

Selina Young

David Fickling Books
OXFORD · NEW YORK

Down by the seashore
Bess and I
stood on the sand
and looked at the sky.

Bess got the hammer.
I got the saw.
We both built a boat
right there on the shore.

I got the needle.
Bess got the thread.
We stitched up a sail
from rags of red.

Bess got the biscuits.
I made the tea.
We both had a sit-down
there by the sea.

I got a compass.
Bess got a chart.
We bought them both
from Captain Bart.

We launched our boat
as the tide went out.
We both gave a wave
and Bart gave a shout.

Over the ocean
Bess and I
sailed to the place
where sea meets sky.

We whistled a chantey.
We waved to a whale.

Bess worked the rudder
and I worked the sail.

We came to the island
marked on the chart.
We searched for the sign
of Captain Bart.

We dug up a chest
so strange and old,
filled with jewels
and gleaming gold.

Pirates chased us
across the bay.
Along came the whale
and scared them away.

We followed the wind
and we rode the foam
until we spied
the shores of home.

Bess got the tools.
I found the wood.
We built us a shack
as best we could.

We made our home
on that same shore.
And we both lived there
forevermore,

singing songs
of far-off seas,
with children sitting
round our knees,

and telling stories
side by side,
"Down by the seashore
once upon a tide . . ."

for Mum & thankyou
all my love Selina x

to Elizabeth, Doris,
Guthrie and Tiggy
from papa Tony with love xxxx

A DAVID FICKLING BOOK

Published by David Fickling Books, an imprint of Random House Children's Books, a division of Random House, Inc., New York

Text copyright © 2004 by Tony Mitton
Illustrations copyright © 2004 by Selina Young

Published simultaneously in Canada by Random House of Canada Limited, Toronto. Originally published in Great Britain by David Fickling Books, an imprint of Random House Children's Books.

www.randomhouse.com/kids

Library of Congress Cataloging-in-Publication Data
Mitton, Tony.
Once upon a tide / Tony Mitton ; illustrated by Selina Young. — 1st American ed.
p.   cm.
SUMMARY: A boy and a girl build a boat and sail off to find Captain Bart's buried treasure.
ISBN 0-385-75100-1 (trade) — ISBN 0-385-75101-X (lib. bdg.)
[1. Sailing—Fiction. 2. Buried treasure—Fiction. 3. Stories in rhyme.] I. Young, Selina, ill. II. Title.
PZ8.3.M685On 2006   [E]—dc22   2005001723

MANUFACTURED IN CHINA
May 2006
10 9 8 7 6 5 4 3 2 1
First American Edition

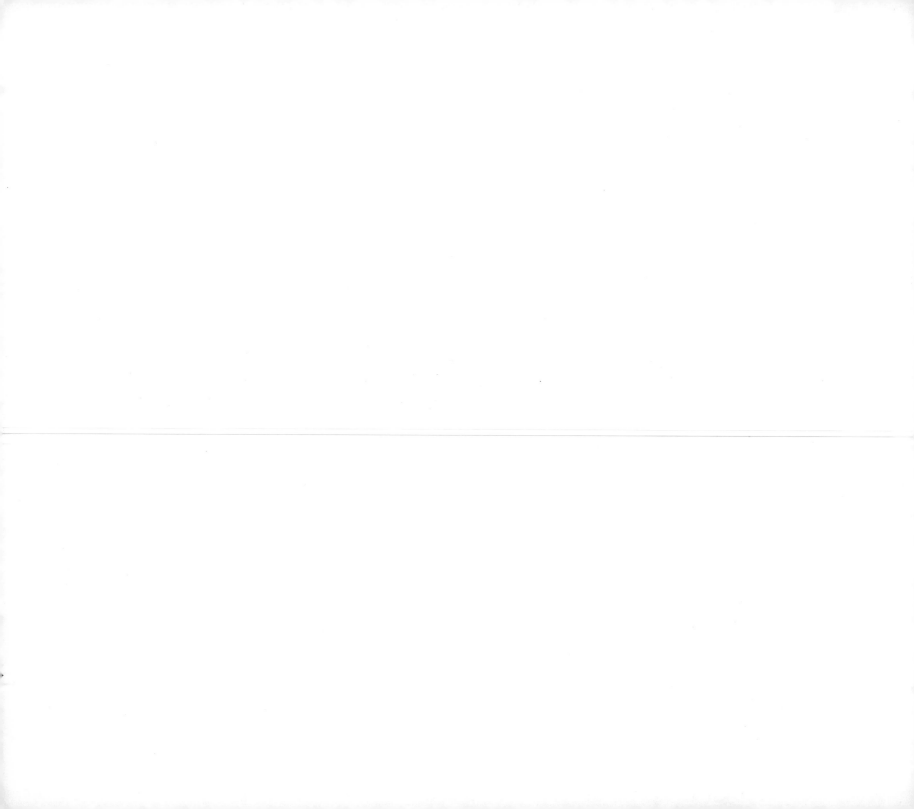